Get Out and Play...
RUGBY!

written by **Rod Smith**
illustrated by **Derry Dillon**

Published 2015

This Series *Get Out and Play . . .*

An imprint of Poolbeg Press Ltd

123 Grange Hill, Baldoyle
Dublin 13, Ireland

Text, layout & design © Poolbeg Press Ltd 2015

A catalogue record for this book is available from the British Library.

ISBN 978 1 78199 924 0

Cover design and illustrations by Derry Dillon
Printed by GPS Colour Graphics Ltd, Alexander Road, Belfast BT6 9HP

Get Out and Play...
RUGBY!

written by **Rod Smith**
illustrated by **Derry Dillon**

This book belongs to

- -

The team I support is

- -

Nine-year-old Oscar Rafferty loved to play video games on his tablet. However, at this particular moment he was running down the street with his Granddad Mick in search of the stolen Golden Whistle.

They were chasing a mysterious black bus, owned by Titus Fortify, the world famous toymaker and video-game creator.

The bus stopped beside Leon and Drake, two of Oscar's friends, who were making their way home after the football match they had all just played with their team, Starchester United.

"Drake! Leon! Don't get on that bus!" Oscar shouted. They couldn't hear him, and the bus left with the boys on board. "Granddad, we have to save them!"

Granddad Mick spotted a motorbike parked on the footpath.

"Get on, Oscar! Put this helmet on!" he shouted as he jumped on himself and produced two helmets from inside his coat. He started the engine by putting his hand over the ignition.

The motorbike sped down the road in pursuit.

"Watch the traffic lights ahead, Granddad – they're turning red! Granddad, look out!"

As the motorbike approached the traffic lights, Granddad Mick raised his hand into the air and the lights magically changed back to green again and they went through safely.

Just ahead, the black bus turned into a large sports stadium.

Granddad Mick stopped the motor bike at the stadium gate.

There was a sign outside: *Open Rugby Tournament Today – Rugby Teams only.*

"We need to get inside," Granddad Mick said.

"But it says rugby teams only."

Granddad Mick waved his hand in the air and suddenly the Starchester United football team appeared.

They looked around, confused.

"I was walking home just a second ago from our football match," said Alice.

"I was with you!" said Nuala.

Mikhail, Jackson, Shane and Henry had a similar story to tell.

"Listen up, everyone," said Oscar. "Titus Fortify has kidnapped Leon and Drake. They're inside these gates!"

"Nobody messes with Starchester players!" Alice declared.

"Oh, it's on!" agreed Mikhail, as he hit his hand with his fist.

"How do we get in?" asked Shane.

"Come with me," said Granddad Mick.

They all walked up to the gate where there was a security guard waiting.

"Team name?" asked the security guard.

"Starchester Lions," replied Granddad Mick. "Look into my eyes. You will add their name to the list now and you will let us through."

"Yes, I will add the name to the list and you may come through," the security guard said, looking dazed.

"You've got to teach me how to do that!" Mikhail said with a laugh as they all entered.

"Alice, you take the team over to the pitch – Oscar and I will try and find Leon and Drake," said Granddad Mick.

Granddad Mick and Oscar soon found the black bus. It had a huge satellite dish on the roof.

"How do we get in?" Oscar asked.

"Why, we knock, of course!"

Granddad Mick knocked on the door.

"*Granddad Mick!*" roared Titus Fortify as he opened the door.

Granddad Mick touched his head and Titus fell back onto a seat, asleep.

Leon and Drake were sitting at the back of the bus at a table, wearing headsets and playing a video game.

Oscar ran down to them.

"Oscar, you've got to play this," Leon said without looking up. "It's called *The Search for the Golden Whistle.*"

"Yes, you really have to play," said Drake as he grabbed Oscar and tried to put a headset over his head.

"What are you doing? Granddad, help!"

Granddad Mick rushed down to the back of the bus, and gently put his hands on Leon and Drake's heads.

Leon and Drake rubbed their eyes and looked around.

"What are we doing here?" asked Drake.

"Nice bus!" said Leon, looking around. "Ooh look, video games!"

"Come on, lads," said Granddad Mick as he helped the boys off the bus. "Let's join the rest of the team."

They ran over to the pitch where they were welcomed by the rest of the Starchester team.

"*Up next, Starchester Lions against the Malberry Maulers,*" said the voice over the loudspeaker.

"We've got Leon and Drake now, so we don't need to play the rugby match," said Granddad Mick.

"This is the same Malberry team we beat at football. I think we can take them, Granddad!" said Oscar. "What do you think, team?"

"No problem!" said Alice.

"Let's do it!" said Henry.

The whole team nodded in agreement.

"I know the ball is oval-shaped but that's all I know – how do we play rugby?" asked Mikhail.

"We'll learn as we play!" shouted Granddad Mick as he joined them on the pitch.

The referee got ready to blow the whistle. Malberry lined up to kick the ball towards Starchester.

"Try and catch it and run with it towards

the Malberry line!" shouted Granddad Mick.

The ball was kicked up in the air and was caught brilliantly by Oscar.

"Run, Oscar!" shouted Leon.

Oscar put his head down and ran straight ahead with the ball.

Wham! He was tackled by three Malberry players and he dropped the ball.

The referee blew the whistle to stop play.

Oscar picked himself slowly off the ground.

"Is that legal?" Henry asked.

"They're allowed to grab you below your neck with their hands," said Granddad Mick.

"This is going to be a very long match!" groaned Shane.

"Scrum to Malberry, ball went forward!" said the referee.

"The ball always has to be passed backwards," Granddad Mick explained. "You can kick the ball forwards, but you have to pass backwards."

"What's a scrum?" asked Nuala.

"It's where we lock arms and put our heads down and push against the other team. One player, called the scrum-half, rolls the ball in the middle between the teams and we try and push them off to win the ball."

"It sounds like a reverse Tug of War!" laughed Drake.

"Arms together, and heave!" Alice instructed as they formed a scrum against Malberry.

The Malberry team were so large they easily pushed the Starchester players down the pitch. The Malberry captain then grabbed the ball and started running towards the goalposts.

"If he gets over the line, it's called a try and he scores five points for the team!" shouted Granddad Mick.

Henry raced over and grabbed the ankle of the Malberry captain who fell to the ground, spilling the ball. Oscar picked up the ball and saw four huge Malberry players running towards him.

"He's going to be flattened!" shouted Leon.

Oscar kicked the ball high in the air and over the heads of the Malberry players. He ran after it as fast as he could and caught it before it landed.

"Stop him!" roared the Malberry captain.

Three of the Malberry players gave chase.

"Dive for the line, Oscar!" shouted Granddad Mick as Oscar ran towards their goalposts.

The Malberry players were just about to catch him when Oscar jumped for the line and touched the ball down.

"Try for Starchester!" shouted the referee. "Conversion to follow."

"Oscar, are you all right?" asked Granddad Mick.

"Never better, Granddad!" laughed Oscar as he stood up.

"Well done, Oscar! Now, Alice, you take the conversion. It's a free shot at goal a team gets after scoring a try. You have to kick the ball over the crossbar. It will get us another two points."

Alice stepped up to take the conversion and it sailed over the crossbar. Seven-nil to Starchester Lions!

"Everyone back to their own side of the pitch now," Granddad Mick said. "Malberry have to restart the match on the halfway line and kick the ball back to us. When you catch the ball you can pass backwards to another player, kick it ahead of you, or kick it out for a lineout throw."

Mikhail jumped up to catch the ball after it was kicked. He passed it backwards to Granddad Mick who caught it and passed it back to Shane. Shane threw it quickly to Nuala who passed it back to Leon who kicked it up the field. Drake, Oscar and Henry ran after the ball, and Henry was just about to pick it up when he was tackled by a Malberry player.

"Penalty to Starchester! Tackling a player who does not have the ball!" shouted the referee.

"This is another free shot at goal – we get three points if we kick this over the crossbar," said Granddad Mick.

Alice lined it up and kicked it over the bar again. Ten-nil to Starchester Lions!

Suddenly Titus Fortify appeared on the sideline.

"Granddad Mick, I have the Golden Whistle!" he shouted as he took a games console out of his pocket. He twisted it between his hands and it broke in two. A golden whistle popped out. He put it to his lips and blew it three times.

All of the adults and children in the rugby stadium and all over the world stopped what they were doing and stood as if frozen.

"Children of the world!" he shouted.
"By the power of the Golden Whistle I
command you to stop what you are doing
and play my wonderful new video game,
The Search for the Golden Whistle!"

Children all over the world grabbed
any device they could and started to play
the video game.

Meanwhile, Titus walked around the
stadium and handed out games consoles
to all of the children.

"Granddad, why does Titus want all of
the children to play his game?" asked Oscar.

Granddad Mick looked at Oscar in surprise. "Oscar! The Golden Whistle has no power over you! Great! Tell me, if you had your tablet, could you see what happens in this game?"

"I think so."

Granddad Mick put his hand inside his coat, produced the tablet and handed it to Oscar. "Start the game and let's see what happens."

Oscar started to play.

"It says I have to find the Golden Whistle and help free the Supervisor and his army so they can rule the world!"

"That's it. He must have found the Supervisor!"

"Golden Whistle? Supervisor? Granddad,

I'm only nine. You're going to have to help me here!" said Oscar.

"Many years ago," said Granddad Mick, "there was a cruel greedy leader called the Supervisor. He and his army forced the people to hand over everything they owned to make him richer. One day he passed some children playing sports outside and he decided they would be ideal to help him dig for gold. As they were small they could fit into tight spaces in the underground mines where the gold could be found. However, the children only wanted to play, so they refused to work for him. The Supervisor asked a magical toymaker Titus Fortify for help. He created an enchanted golden

whistle. When the Supervisor blew the whistle three times, all of the children stopped what they were doing and obeyed his order to go down the mines."

"That's so cruel!"

"Yes, but they didn't know that one of the children had magical powers. He was able to reverse the magic spell of the whistle. So the next time the Supervisor blew the whistle, the Supervisor, the whistle, and his army were transported to a different space and time. They were never seen again."

"So how did Titus find the whistle?"

"He must have got it from the Supervisor through the video game somehow."

"It must have been sent through the Wi-Fi signal on the gaming device!" Oscar said. "Titus must have been able to create some type of energy link between himself and the Supervisor."

"Well, aren't you clever, Oscar!" declared Titus as he arrived back. "Transporting a whistle is one thing. You need a much stronger energy link to transport people!"

"That's why you have every child on the planet playing the game. The more children who play, the stronger the energy link becomes!" said Oscar.

"That's right, and it's working!" shouted Titus as he pointed up into the air. "Here they come!"

Large numbers of energy bubbles started to form in the air. The shape of a person began to appear in each bubble.

"Why do they all have beards?" asked Oscar, as he looked up.

"Only the mightiest and most worthy are allowed to grow a beard," replied Titus as he sadly stroked his moustache.

Oscar pulled Granddad Mick aside. "Granddad," he whispered, "those energy

bubbles are being created within the game. I think we can use the game to destroy the bubbles."

"Great idea, Oscar. It might not stop them, but it would slow them down. Then, if we can destroy the Wi-Fi signal, that should break the connection completely. We just need to find the source."

"The satellite dish on the roof of the black bus!" shouted Oscar. "That must be it!"

"Leave that to me!" said Granddad Mick. "You keep playing. Titus is so busy looking up at those energy bubbles, he's ignoring us, so let's do it!"

A very large energy bubble started to form. It was the Supervisor himself!

"I have returned! I shall rule again and finally have my revenge on Grandad Mick!" boomed his voice from the sky.

"Yes, my lord. I knew if he thought the Golden Whistle was stolen he would try to find it!" said Titus.

"Titus sent the note saying the Golden Whistle was stolen!" gasped Oscar.

"Titus Fortify, you have served me well. From this day on you will be permitted to grow the beard of distinction!"

"Thank you, magnificent one!" replied Titus as he bowed his head.

Oscar concentrated on playing the game on his tablet and started to destroy the energy bubbles.

Slowly but surely the Supervisor's energy bubble started to grow smaller, while the other energy bubbles around him started to fade.

"What's happening?" roared Titus.

Granddad Mick raced back to Oscar.

"Cover your ears!" he said.

Suddenly there was a loud bang and a blinding flash of light as the black bus exploded into the air in thousands of pieces and turned into harmless black feathers as it fell back to earth.

"I never liked that black bus!" said
Granddad Mick.

The energy bubbles disappeared.

"*Noooooooo!*" shouted Titus as the image
of the Supervisor faded.

"Quick, Oscar, grab my hand!" shouted
Granddad Mick.

In an instant, they disappeared from the rugby stadium and reappeared in Oscar's house.

"What happened? Where are the rest of the team?" asked Oscar.

"They are all safely back in their homes."

"Did you think you would escape that easily? You have ruined my plans!" roared a voice at the door.

It was Titus! He pointed a magic video-game controller at Oscar and Granddad Mick. They were both rooted to the spot.

"Granddad Mick, I will deal with you later. Now, Oscar, the Golden Whistle had no effect on you. Could it be that you have magical powers too?" Titus stroked his moustache. "I can't possibly allow that. Would you like to see how the rapid-fire button works on my magic game-controller?"

Oscar closed his eyes and braced himself.

"HOW DARE YOU THREATEN MY GRANDSON!" roared Granddad Mick with such force that the spell was broken.

Titus pushed a button on his magic controller and disappeared.

But not before Oscar was able to grab something from him.

"Look, Granddad! I've got the Golden Whistle!"

"Well done, Oscar! Let's put the whistle in a safe place."

He put it into the inside pocket of his coat. The whole coat shone brightly for a moment, and then went back to normal.

"Granddad, do I have magic?" asked Oscar.

"Every day with you, Oscar, is a day of magic. Now come on, let's get the Starchester team back together. We have a rugby tournament to finish."

And they finished in great style by winning the trophy!

Rugby Facts

1823   William Webb Ellis invents the game
by picking up the ball during a game
of football at Rugby school.

1854   The oldest rugby club, Dublin University
Football Club, is formed.

1886   The International Rugby Board
is formed (IRB).

1892   An oval ball is used for the first time in
matches. They are oval because they are
made from pigs' bladders which are oval
when inflated.

1924   USA win the gold medal at the last rugby
tournament played at the Olympics, so
they are the current Olympic champions!

1948   Ireland wins the Grand Slam in the
Five Nations Championship.

1978	Munster becomes the first Irish team to beat New Zealand, winning 12-0.
1987	New Zealand wins the first Rugby World Cup.
1995	Toulouse wins the first Rugby Union European Cup.
2009	Ireland wins the Grand Slam in the Six Nations Championship.
2014-15	Ireland wins the Six Nations Championship for two years in a row.

A Try is worth 5 points in rugby, but used to be worth no points. When a team touched the ball down over the goal line they were given the chance to "try" to score points by kicking the ball over the crossbar.

The whistle used to kick off the first game in every World Cup was first used in 1905.

Rugby is the national sport of three countries – Wales, Madagascar and New Zealand.

Ireland has 4 players who have played 100 or more matches: Brian O'Driscoll, Ronan O'Gara, John Hayes and Paul O'Connell.

The haka is a traditional dance or challenge of the New Zealand Maori people which is performed by the New Zealand team before each match.

HIGHEST SCORERS

Dan Carter of New Zealand (also known as "the All Blacks") is the highest points-scorer ever.

Ronan O'Gara of Ireland is the highest Irish points-scorer ever.

WORLD CUP WINNERS

New Zealand, Australia, South Africa and England have all won the World Cup.

IRISH TEAMS

There are four provincial teams in Ireland: Leinster, Munster, Ulster and Connacht.

Leinster, Munster and Ulster have all won the European Cup.

CONNACHT

ULSTER

MUNSTER

LEINSTER